KT-151-627

THIS WALKER BOOK BELONGS TO:

_____

_____

_____

For Robyn – J.E.
For Hugo – V.C.

LIBRARY SERVICES FOR SCHOOLS	
03288891	
Bertrams	08.09.07
	£5.99

First published in Great Britain 2005
by Walker Books Ltd
87 Vauxhall Walk, London SE11 5HJ

This edition published 2005

2 4 6 8 10 9 7 5 3

Text © 2004 Jonathan Emmett
Illustrations © 2004 Vanessa Cabban

The right of Jonathan Emmett and Vanessa Cabban to be identified
as author and illustrator respectively of this work has been asserted by them
in accordance with the Copyright, Designs and Patents Act 1988

You can find out more about Jonathan Emmett's
books by visiting his website at www.scribblestreet.co.uk

This book has been typeset in Beta Bold

Printed in China

All rights reserved. No part of this book may
be reproduced, transmitted or stored in an information
retrieval system in any form or by any means, graphic,
electronic or mechanical, including photocopying,
taping and recording, without prior written permission
from the publisher.

British Library Cataloguing in Publication Data:
a catalogue record for this book is available
from the British Library

ISBN-13: 978-1-84428-521-1
ISBN-10: 1-84428-521-9

www.walkerbooks.co.uk

No Place Like Home

Jonathan Emmett

illustrated by Vanessa Cabban

WALKER BOOKS
AND SUBSIDIARIES
LONDON · BOSTON · SYDNEY · AUCKLAND

"Hot-diggerty!"
said Mole, as he climbed
out of the ground one morning.
It was a beautiful day.
The sun was shining.
And there were flowers everywhere.
Suddenly Mole's burrow seemed
very small and dark and dull.
"Why should I live underground,"
Mole said to himself,
"when I could live
somewhere BIG
and BRIGHT
and BEAUTIFUL instead!"

And Mole
set off in search
of a new home.

He hadn't
gone far when
he came across
Hedgehog.

"Hello, Mole,"
said Hedgehog. "Where are you off to?"

"I'm looking for a new home," explained Mole.
"Somewhere
BIG and
BRIGHT and
BEAUTIFUL."

"I know just the place!"
said Hedgehog.
"Follow me!"

"So what do you think?"
asked Hedgehog,
as they crawled into a hollow log.
Mole tried to feel at home
in the log, but the wind
was whistling right
through it.

"Well,"
said Mole, shivering,
"it is very BIG – but it's too drafty
for me. I'd like somewhere
a little more snug."

"What's up?"
asked Squirrel.

Mole and Hedgehog
had just crawled
out of the log
when they saw
Squirrel.

"I'm looking
for a new home,"
explained Mole.
"Somewhere
BRIGHT
and BEAUTIFUL."

"And SNUG,"
added
Hedgehog.

"I know just the place!"
said Squirrel.
"Follow me!"

"So what do you think?"
said Squirrel, as Mole clambered
into an empty bird's nest.

Mole tried to feel
at home in the nest. But he was
too afraid of falling out.

"Well," he said, "it is very BRIGHT –
but it's too dangerous for me.
I'd like somewhere a little
more safe."

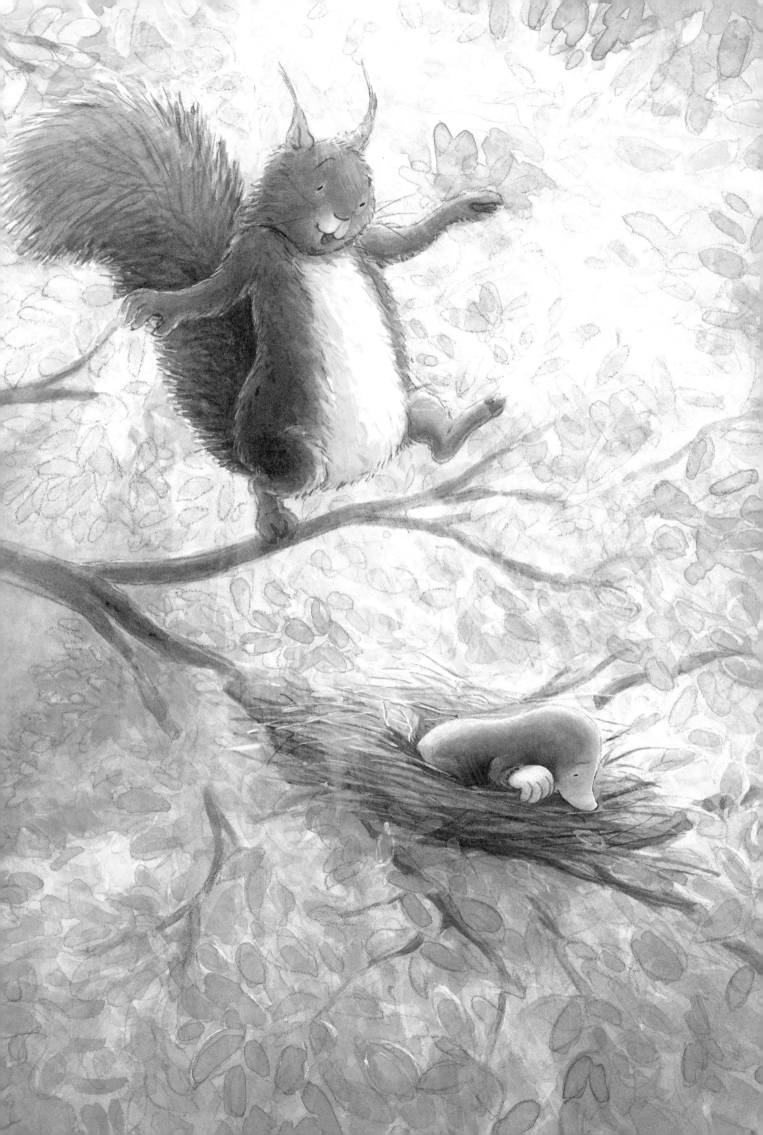

Hedgehog, Squirrel and Mole
had just climbed back to the ground
when Rabbit came bounding up.

"What's happening?" asked Rabbit.

"I'm looking for a new home," explained Mole. "Somewhere BEAUTIFUL."

"And SNUG," added Hedgehog.

"And SAFE," added Squirrel.

"I know just the place!" said Rabbit.

Rabbit led Mole,
    Squirrel and Hedgehog
        to a little stream.

"Over here!" she said,
hopping easily
from stone to stone.

"So what do you think?"
said Rabbit, as they scrambled
into a hollow beside
a sparkling waterfall.

Mole tried to feel at home
in the hollow. But he kept
getting splashed.

"Well," he said, "it is very
BEAUTIFUL –
but it's too wet for me.
I'd like somewhere
a little more dry."

It was getting late and Mole
still hadn't found his new home.

"I didn't think it would
be this difficult," sighed Mole.

"Don't worry. We'll find somewhere," said Rabbit.

"We just need to give
it some thought," said Squirrel.

So they all sat down and thought,
and thought, and thought, until...

"I know just the place,"
said Mole.

He led Squirrel, Hedgehog
and Rabbit back across the woodland
to a familiar-looking hole.

"But this is your OLD home!"
said Rabbit, Hedgehog and Squirrel.

"I know," said Mole happily.

"Isn't it WONDERFUL?

It's not BIG or BRIGHT or BEAUTIFUL.

But it feels

just right to me."

It was dark outside, and a storm
was sweeping across the woodland.
But everyone was very
comfortable down
in Mole's burrow.

"It's so SNUG,"
said Hedgehog.

"And SAFE,"
said Squirrel.

"And DRY,"
said Rabbit.

"Yes," said Mole
contentedly.
"There's no place
like home!"

WALKER BOOKS is the world's leading
independent publisher of children's books.
Working with the best authors and illustrators
we create books for all ages, from babies
to teenagers – books your child will
grow up with and always remember. So…

FOR THE BEST CHILDREN'S BOOKS,
LOOK FOR THE BEAR